CAFFEINATED
Short Stories

Theresa Jacobs, Maxine Hernandez, William R. Bartlett,
Kate Hampton, Josephine Go and Lucy Lombos

Copyright

This is a Collection of Short Stories, published by Lombosco Publications-Canada.

Date Published: May 11, 2023

Book Cover Designed by: David Enriquez, Jr. from the Philippines.

Note: The authors' names on the book's front cover were listed based on their submission dates. The last name is the primary author.

Table of Contents

Introduction

Winter. It's the time of long nights, so it's all darkness and coldness. Snow and ice for three months are a common, natural sight. It's a difficult time to go out, albeit it's chilly fun for some sporty individuals. It's also the time to catch up and have quality time with the family at home. For me, it's the time to read books, write short stories and drink coffee.

On December 15, 2022, I made my black coffee. I stared at it. As if its steam formed stars that twinkled. Imaginably, my mind welcomed the glow and my eyes enjoyed watching the flickers closely. "Was I dreaming?" I asked myself. Then, all of a sudden, a flash of an idea came. Coffee! That hot stuff made me think of it as my writing prompt.

"Hey, write something about me!" My coffee spoke and called my attention.

"Why not?" I replied. That was an inviting inkling.

Such a steamy-starry invitation happened. Eventually, Canadian author Theresa Jacobs gave me her supportive "yes" to this coffee writing project. She promised to brew the idea first. Not too long on January 18, 2023, she emailed her fantastic short story to me.

While writing and developing my own story, Maxine Hernandez from California also said a sweet yes to this project. On January 29, 2023, she sent me her beautiful short story.

Recalling from that day on, I contacted the following authors (in alphabetical order)- William R. Bartlett, Josephine Go, and Kate Hampton. I kept in touch with them and followed them up persistently. Thank God, later, they assured me that they would write something with a similar theme. I appreciated all their excellent responses. Moreover, I mentioned all their names on the book's Acknowledgment Page based on the dates of their submission.

On a snowy day of January 31, 2023, this book that landed on your hand and before your eyes finally obtained its title- C A F F E I N A T E D Short Stories.

The first short story in this anthology, penned by Theresa Jacobs, is a speculative fiction with a twilight essence.

The next tale, written by Maxine Hernandez, is an interesting fable-like short story with anthropomorphized animals as characters, conveying a moral to the readers.

The third addition, authored by William R. Bartlett, tells the readers a love story between a man and his wife, and the strength of the bond between them.

Worded by Kate Hampton, the fourth contribution describes a dream that changed the main character's relationship with someone who truly loves and takes care of her.

The fifth account, prepared by Josephine Go, depicts an ardent longing for a family, and it is considered a quest narrative that works toward a goal.

And the last but not the least narrative, crafted by the lead author, is blended with a non-linear reflection. In the occurrence of conflict, it ends with a shocking life drama solely borne from the author's creative imagination.

Good book, good reading over a cup of coffee!

- Lucy Lombos
Lead Author

1.

"Grindhouse"

By Theresa Jacobs

Ice pelts shot from invisible clouds in the darkness, stabbing my exposed face. I sighed, calling into the air, "Another deserved punishment for your death, Doris. Go ahead, Gods of the sky, kill me slowly. I shouldn't have lived through the crash."

My frozen feet burned with every step in the icy slush. The pain wasn't enough to distract me from my guilt. The day Doris died behind the wheel, no thanks to me, I vowed to never drive again. The hour-long walk from my weekly AA meeting to home in the dead of winter was a mere stipend of the punishment I should receive.

Not yet ready to return to my soulless apartment, I took an unfamiliar turn, walking past shops closed for the night. The windows were filled with bright sparkly trinkets and clothing that cried out to be bought, worn, and loved.

I only gave them a passing glance until a faint glow gave me pause. Lifting my head, I saw an opaque window with the name "Grindhouse," painted in inky black letters. A slight movement inside urged me to enter.

Opening the door, warm steamy air and the soothing scent of freshly brewed coffee greeted me. Leaving the bitter snap of winter's night air behind me, I stamped the snow off my boots and removed my hat while spying a cozy-looking table at the back of the small coffeehouse. My first thought, *Doris would have loved this place.*

The woman—who appeared either 50ish or overworked and tired, it wasn't my place to judge—lifted a dark pot in my direction.

I nodded, making my way to the two-person booth near a window. I was the only patron in the small space and I glanced at the clock, shocked to learn the time had slipped past ten o'clock pm.

"How late are you open?" I asked as the waitress set a plain white cup in front of me. I noted her name tag read, Flo.

Flo's eyes stayed on the cup. "As late as we need be," she said.

That's an odd response, I thought and watched her not look at me. Her age truly was unidentifiable. Her skin tone might be olive in the sunlight, but in the dim corner, it was riddled with shadow and absorbed an amber hue from the bad fluorescent bulbs. Fine lines traced her eyes and a smattering of grey wove through her thick black hair. She was the polar opposite of my fair-skinned, red-haired Doris.

Without lifting her eyes, Flo said, "Watch the coffee, Phil."

Taken aback, I wanted to ask her how she knew my name, except the rising aromatic steam and the gentle lap of liquid hitting the bottom of my cup drew my eyes down. The room swirled around in a vortex. I grabbed the table's edge, wanting to look away, focus on Flo again, or stare at the ceiling—anything would be better than this stomach-rolling wave of vertigo. I had no control over my body. I lost all substance as I turned into particles and was sucked into the dark, roiling liquid stream.

~~~~~

"Whoa!" I grabbed my head and closed my eyes.

"Are you okay? Phil? Phil?"

Doris's soft fingers wrapped around my wrist and I reached for her shoulder, blinking. Her emerald eyes
~~~~~

swam into view and I smiled. "Touch of vertigo, I guess," I said.

She gave my hand a squeeze. "We can call off the party tonight if you're not up to it."

"Are you kidding! I'd wear a hazmat suit if I had pneumonia to make sure your fortieth birthday still happened."

"You spoil me too much, Phil. Will you still love me when I'm old, fat and crotchety?"

Lunging up, I grabbed her around the waist, spilling us both onto the couch. She giggled, her fist play pounding on my back. I planted wet kisses on her cheeks and neck. "I'll love you when I'm old, fat and crotchety!"

We snuggled a few minutes more before she left me to get herself ready for the party. I headed to the washroom for a shower and shave. It was best to be clean-shaven prior to a long night. I smiled at the lilting melody she sang from the next room and looked at myself in the mirror. "You're the luckiest man alive, Phil. How does such a beautiful, kind, generous creature love this ugly mug?"

"If you're ugly, I have bad taste!" Doris yelled from the bedroom.

I chuckled. "I thought you were busy singing," I called back. "How can you listen to me and sing at the same time?"

"I'm amazing, remember?" she replied, laughing.

"That you are, my love. That you are."

I picked up the tune she sang, hummed along, and stepped into the shower.

~~~~~

I watched Doris glow in our friends and family's love and adoration. Always humble, she waved off cheers to her. Even though it was her birthday celebration, she thrived on being around those she loved, not all the shining praise to the wonder that was her. The party wore late into the night, drinks flowed, people danced themselves to exhaustion and laughter rang through the air. The crowds thinned as time drew closer to daylight. I couldn't have asked for a better party.

"Happy birthday again, sweety," Rachel, Doris's best friend, said, squeezing her tight.

"Thanks for coming, hon. Are you two cabbing it?"
~~~~~

"Absolutely! I'm seeing three of you," Rachel laughed, nudging her husband to run and grab their coats. "Love you, doll. Lunch on Thursday?"

Doris kissed Rachel's cheek. "Wouldn't miss it for the world. Love you."

"Bye, guys!" I called from behind them. "Be safe."

"You too," Rachel yelled back as they exited.

"Ready?" I asked, taking Doris's hand.

She looked around, assessing the mess we'd left or checking for stragglers. I didn't know and pulled her towards the doors.

"That was the best party ever, Phil. Thank you, thank you, thank you!"

I helped her into her coat and slipped mine on, bringing the keys from my pocket. "Anything for you, my love, you know that."

Her eyes fell on my hand. "We'd better call a cab."

"Nah, I'm good, sweetheart. I stopped drinking a couple of hours ago."

She grabbed my cheeks, stood on her tiptoes, and planted a hard kiss on my lips. "You're the best!"

"Mmm, I'll expect more of that when we get home," I said, giving her a tight hug. I led her out to the car, opened and closed her door and proceeded to the driver's side. Sliding behind the wheel, I gave her a wink and stuck the key into the ignition. The overwhelming sense of déjà vu gave me pause. A rush of electricity rolled from my head to my feet, accompanied by sudden nausea and a sense of doom.

"Phil?" Doris asked.

"Huh?" I blinked and, realizing my mouth was hanging open, closed it.

"Are you sure you're alright? Maybe we should get you a physical this week."

"Nah, it was just déjà vu."

"Oh, I hate it when that happens. It's so creepy. Don't you think? I mean, how can we have a sense of doing something before that we haven't actually done yet?"

The conversation rambled into fate, destiny and the unusual things in life when suddenly, the world went black. My head spun. When my view changed, I didn't have time to think about stopping the car or slowing down.

I was no longer driving South along Route Four in our silver Elantra with Doris beside me. The view before had altered to North Route Four, the direction we'd driven hours before toward the party. Expect the hood out the window before my eyes were higher off the ground, Red, and that of a Jeep. The hands upon the wheel were not mine. I have long, slender fingers with no hair and manicured nails. These hands were short, thick, hairy, and dirty, like those of a mechanic, perhaps. A fat smoldering cigar sat between two fingers.

I most certainly did not smoke. I tried to move my fingers and nothing. My head, nothing. Blink nothing. I noted headlights crest a hill on the opposite side of the road. The cigar tumbled from the driver's grip and bounced off the console, landing on the passenger side floor. "Son 'of-A!" a deep voice growled.

The on-coming car grew closer. Close enough for me to see the familiar hood of a silver Elantra and the two faces behind the windshield—Doris and I.

How can it be?

If I had control of the mouth, it'd be agape.

The body I could not control leaned right, reaching for the cigar. The left hand on the wheel jerked.

I saw Doris looking at me—the silver Elantra driving me—and laughed. Neither of us had time to see the Jeep run straight into our car.

A blink later and the world resumed in darkness.

~~~~~

My body tilted sideways. My vertigo worsened and my stomach let go. Hot liquid spewed from my mouth and I hit the floor on my hands and knees. The cramps stopped as fast as they'd arrived and I stared at the black-and-white checkered floor beneath me.

I turned away from the milky liquid of my stomach contents, noticing a sensible flat-heeled shoe and the puffy ankle above it. A hand reached out, and I took it.

Flo stood behind the booth and helped me to my feet, holding a napkin. Stupefied, I curled it in my fingers, wiped my chin, and stared into her obsidian eyes.

"It wasn't my fault," I muttered.

Placing a hand on my back, not releasing the one in her hand, Flo led me toward the door. I panicked and halted, forcing her to stop with me. "Do it again! I can
~~~~~

save her now! I know what happened. I have to go back!" I tried to turn, but the woman held me in place.

"It's over, Phil. We can't change what happened. We can only show you a better way. You can let go now and love again."

"NO! I can't! Doris is everything to me. Can't you see that?"

The door opened on its own. Flo pressed my hat onto my head. "Live Phil. Live," she said and shoved me out into the blooming twilight. The snow had stopped and the tangerine skyline appeared precisely as it had on my last morning with Doris.

I spun back. I had to try again, to the renter, to go back, but the café was gone.

"Wha—"

I moved to the brick wall, placing my hand where a double-paned glass door had been on seconds before. I stood back, taking in a broader view. The entire building was comprised of brick. There were no windows and no doors.

Did that really happen?

I checked myself over. I wasn't wet, so I hadn't fallen and hit my head. I did notice the pit of despair I'd been hoarding for the past year no longer weighed on my heart. A smile touched my lips.

"I'll always love you, Doris," I said and headed home humming the last tune Doris had sung.

It wasn't my fault after all. I think I can live with that.

~~~~~

Janet couldn't stop the tears from leaking, even though her mother died when she was only six years old. She'd forever carry the guilt of leaving her pieces of Lego on the floor. *If only I'd done as she asked and picked them up, she thought for the millionth time.* The mantra triggered the image of her mom stepping on a sharp piece and crying out in pain before tumbling to the carpeted floor, where she lay still and never moved again. That was the most vivid nightmare, which had lived in her every waking moment since that fateful day.

Lost in her own thoughts, a door opened on her left, the bells above it jangling and she startled. "Oh," she uttered, clutching her coat.

A waitress wearing a tag that read Flo smiled and motioned her inside.
~~~~~

The warmer interior air wafted out, carrying the unmistakable scent of fresh coffee and the urge to go in and partake in that deliciousness prompted Janet to enter.

"Thank you, Flo," she said, entering the empty yet cozy space.

2.

"Coffee and Dumplings"

By Maxine Hernandez

On a cold and snowy day, Jeff, the coyote and Todd, the honey badger, trotted alongside each other. The forest floor was covered in snow and the trees held no leaves aside from random lumps of snow on their branches.

"Do you know what sounds good right now, Todd? Some steaming hot coffee and dumplings! Coffee brewed from freshly ground coffee beans!" Jeff mused.

Todd grunted in agreement, "I might have some coffee in my burrow. I am not sure about dumplings, though."

"My favorite is coffee brewed with chicory or cardamom. The spices give the coffee such a great flavor," Jeff, the coyote, added.

"I love mine with condensed milk. It makes the coffee so rich!" Todd, the honey badger, replied.

With a common goal in mind, the two friends padded along, leaving parallel footprints on the white snow.

As the duo approached the honey badger's burrow, the skies threatened to give more snow. The burrow is located at the base of an enormous live oak. Its foliage is all but gone for the winter season. The ground by the burrow is covered with snow, dried leaves and acorns; the front door is pillared by large roots that somehow grew wide apart from each other.

"Let's go inside and get some coffee!" Todd exclaimed excitedly.

Inside the sparsely furnished burrow, an old cast iron stove stood in the corner of the kitchen. Jeff approached the stove and started a fire. Grabbing a kettle, Jeff fills it up with water for the stove.

"This shouldn't take long at all!" said the coyote.

After setting the kettle on the stove, the coyote noticed his honey badger friend frantically going through every cupboard and pantry in the burrow.

"What are you looking for?" Jeff asked Todd.

"I can't seem to find the coffee! I thought I saw a bag here a couple of days ago," Todd cried.

Deciding to help his friend look for the coffee, Jeff looked through the cupboards and pantry for a second time.

"Yep, I don't think you have any coffee, Todd."

"Darn! I was looking forward to a cup on this cold and dreary morning," Todd said sadly.

Jeff sniffed and felt an idea pop up in his head.

"I know what we can do! Mrs. Cintas, the alligator, might have some coffee. She lives just over the hill by the lake and I know she loves coffee so much! Plus, I see her buy bags of it in town. Perhaps she can lend us some coffee!" Jeff proclaimed happily.

"Mrs. Cintas always makes me work whenever I ask something of her. Perhaps not today, it looks like it is about to snow. I wouldn't want to be caught in the blizzard," Todd commented.

"What kind of work could keep us from having some delicious coffee, though? I would happily trade a little bit of my time for a cup! Come on, it won't be that bad, and we'd be helping Mrs. Cintas since she lives by herself," Jeff offered.

Todd seemed to agree and said, "Oh, alright, I guess we can work quickly and we might be able to beat the afternoon blizzard."

Taking the kettle off the stove, the two friends quickly donned thick jackets and heavy work boots before they headed out in the stormy weather.

"We'll be back before the first snowflake hits this oak tree!" Jeff stated as if it was a challenge.

"I hope so. The skies look angry as it is," was Todd's reply.

Indeed, the skies were gray and the wind was beginning to pick up.

The two friends started walking through the wintry forest and hoped for the best. It was not a far walk to Mrs. Cintas' Lake, but it was not an easy trek through the snow. Jeff, the coyote, was wading through snow that reached his thighs. Todd, the honey badger, was covered in snow all the way to his chest.

"It shouldn't be long. The lake is just over the hill!" Jeff huffed, eyeing his friend, who seemed to struggle to keep pace.

The duo persevered to the top of the hill and sat on the summit upon reaching it. The land opened up to a vast, snow-covered valley in front of them, the center of which is a frozen lake. A steep mountain range bordered the area, and a sleeping evergreen forest stretched as far as the eyes could see.

Todd's gaze hovered over a small patch of marshland on the southern edge of the lake, closest to the hill they were sitting on. In the middle of the marshland stood a small cottage by the lake's shore. The pair did not waste any time in making their way down the hill. Catching their breath, they started down the path to the cottage.

Mrs. Cintas, the alligator, lived alone by herself in a tiny cottage by the lake. The humble abode held itself well through the years. Stone and mortar made up the walls and foundations of the cottage, and the snow covered the fine straw roof.

Jeff and Todd approached the cottage. Firewood was stacked high by the western wall. In certain patches of the yard, snow crocus sprouted out from under the snow. The rest of the shrubbery and foliage were in hibernation. A few rose bushes stood defoliated, asleep until the first warmth of spring. Herb pots lay empty, picked clean and fertilized with a layer of mulch for the next crop.

Jeff and Todd approached the front door. Jeff stood by the doorway and knocked.

"Hold on. I'll be right there!" Mrs. Cintas called. The door opened and a stout and friendly alligator answered the door. Mrs. Cintas wore a plain house dress, over which she had a pristine white apron that rivaled the wearer's charm.

"Hello, Mrs. Cintas! How are you doing today on this fine winter morning?" Jeff asked in a way that showed admiration and respect.

"I am just fabulous, thank you! I spent all morning making dumplings for my social club this evening. What brings you both here today?" the alligator asked, appearing curious.

"Well, Jeff and I were about to make coffee and realized we didn't have any. We were wondering if you had some to spare?" Todd asked rather sheepishly.

"I sure do! Come on in before you catch a chill!" Mrs. Cintas opened the door wider and motioned for the two friends to come inside.

It was a neat little cottage that was bigger inside than it looked outside. The walls were painted a calming cream color, lined with wooden shelves full of books. A warm and inviting hearth kept the one-room cottage warm and cozy. By the hearth were two stately armchairs with a round table in between. The large, solid wood dining table stood opposite the fireplace, lined with trays of freshly made dumplings. The wood fire and the aroma of the dumplings made the two friends wish they had some coffee to go along with the experience.

As Jeff and Todd found cozy spots in the comfort of the armchairs, Mrs. Cintas busied herself in the kitchen. She was opening up all her cupboards in search of something.

"Oh dear, I don't believe I have any more coffee... but I can look in my storage basement under the cottage," Mrs. Cintas explained.

Jeff and Todd exchanged worried looks with each other.

"We can help you look. Just let us know what needs to be done!" Todd offered.

"Thank you, Todd. Come outside with me so we can look in the basement," Mrs. Cintas opened the door and led the way.

Outside, the entrance to the basement was buried under a couple of feet of snow.

"We'll have to shovel all that out to get to the basement," Todd said.

"I have some shovels if you are willing to help me shovel all of this snow away from the doorway," offered Mrs. Cintas.

She walked over to a small shed and produced two shovels for Jeff and Todd. Driven by their desire for a warm cup of freshly brewed coffee, they accepted the shovels from Mrs. Cintas and began digging. The two did not have time to complain, for it was indeed freezing outside, but neither could forget about the coffee. As the two friends dug, Mrs. Cintas disappeared into the house and left the two friends by themselves.

"I told you she always finds something for me to do before giving me anything," Todd softly grumbled.

"Todd, think about that delicious cup of coffee you can have later when we clear all this snow. And besides, Mrs. Cintas couldn't have shoveled all of this snow by herself because of her bad knees," Jeff responded.

"You're right, just a little bit more. I think I just hit the basement doors," Todd said as he plunged the shovel into the snow.

Clearing the remaining snow with their mitted paws, the basement doors revealed themselves. Jeff and Todd called over to Mrs. Cintas for the key to unlock the door.

Mrs. Cintas dropped the keys in the snow while trying to open the basement doors.

"Oh, curse these rheumy hands!" Mrs. Cintas cried, clearly distraught. The honey badger quickly responded and dove in to retrieve the keys.

"Here you go, Mrs. Cintas!" Todd said as he handed the keys to Mrs. Cintas.

"Oh, thank you so much!" And just like that, the trio found themselves descending into the basement. Mrs. Cintas lit some lamps on the walls and the basement gave up its contents. The basement itself was cut away from the bedrock on which the foundation of the cottage stood.

There was no heat source, so the three friends could see the fog of their breath from the cold. Bare rock walls were lined with wooden shelves holding various supplies: Wheels of cheese, sacks of grain and flour, bags of sugar and salt, canned goods, bushels of potatoes and carrots, whole legs of ham and sausages, amongst other things. On the clean stone floor were various other household items; tools that were not needed on a daily basis, spare plates and cutlery for hosting dinner parties, holiday decorations, and boxes of still more things unseen. Drying herbs hung from the wood beams supporting the ceiling.

Mrs. Cintas went straight to the far eastern corner of the room and opened a cupboard.

"There's the good stuff!" she beamed.

Jeff and Todd crowded behind her and stared in amazement at the sacks of whole-bean coffee piled on top of one another.

"Would you please help me get a sack of this coffee upstairs? Somebody usually does this for me on the weekends because of my bad knee. But nobody came last weekend because of the blizzard," Mrs. Cintas asked both Jeff and Todd, motioning with her hands.

"Of course, we'll help you get this coffee sack upstairs! You don't need to worry at all, Mrs. Cintas!" Todd volunteered.

"Oh, thank you so much! With the two of you here, you can help me retrieve at least two sacks of coffee so I will be set for at least the better part of a month!" Ms. Cintas suggested before she disappeared on top of the stairway.

"Absolutely!" called Todd.

"Jeff, I'll take this sack and you can take another one with you," Todd said to Jeff, turning his head and seeing that his friend already got a sack of delicious coffee beans resting on his right shoulder.

"One step ahead of you!" Jeff reported. Both coyote and honey badger, each carrying linen bags full of coffee beans, made their way back into the alligator's cottage.

"Oh, thank you so much! You don't know how much you two helped me out!" Mrs. Cintas exclaimed with glee while giving the two friends a small applause. "You two just take a seat and I will brew some of this coffee," Mrs. Cintas motioned for the two friends to sit by the fire.

The armchairs were warmed by their proximity to the fire and comforted both Jeff and Todd. Mrs. Cintas chatted with Jeff and Todd as the two caught a whiff of the aroma of freshly ground coffee. Mrs. Cintas kept speaking as she took a boiling kettle from the stove and poured the hot water on the freshly ground coffee beans. The old alligator let the grounds steep in hot water, never forgetting the rare company she had sitting by the hearth. Finally, she deftly pressed the beans from the hot water using an old-fashioned coffee press.

"We are happy to help out, Mrs. Cintas! We will see about stopping by more often to help you out," replied Jeff.

Just as Jeff and Todd were having a lull in the conversation, Mrs. Cintas came by the hearth with a tray. Three small cups, the coffee press, a small bowl of sweetened condensed milk and a steaming plate of dumplings.

The coyote and the honey badger took on the sight and the aroma and thought about how the whole thing would taste. Their mouths watered and they looked up to Mrs. Cintas with a look of appreciation. Mrs. Cintas set the tray down on the table between Jeff and Todd.

"This looks great! Thank you!" "Wow!" the two spoke almost at the same time.

The alligator took a chair from the dining table and sat between the coyote and the honey badger, proudly surveying the enthusiasm as the two devoured her homemade dumplings and freshly brewed coffee. Jeff was the first to take a sip of the coffee. He was satisfied. Notes of chicory floated on his palate, cradled by the sweet velvet of the condensed milk.

"You added chicory in there!" Jeff cried admiringly.

"Yes! The coffee merchant gave me a bag of roasted chicory root. I am yet to discover the correct ratio of chicory to grounds." Mrs. Cintas stated in a shy tone.

"Oh, but it is perfect!" Todd countered with gentleness.

The two happily tucked in and started eating. Mrs. Cintas busied herself with her knitting and had her own fill of coffee and dumplings. Quiet moments would lead to fervent conversation and then vice-versa. All three were having a great time by the fire.

Jeff and Todd finished their third cup of coffee and about their eleventh dumpling as Mrs. Cintas concluded her narration. She had been sharing some news from beyond the borders of their realm.

The fire had turned into hot embers and Jeff and Todd decided it was time to go. Todd added more wood to the hearth to keep it going for Mrs. Cintas.

Both thanked Mrs. Cintas and in turn, she gave them each a bag of blended coffee grounds and roasted chicory. She also handed each one a can of condensed milk.

"I hope you two have your own coffee presses to make this with at home!" Mrs. Cintas chimed, with just a touch of concern in her voice. With another round of appreciation and a promise to come back soon, Jeff, the coyote and Todd, the honey badger, bid farewell to Mrs. Cintas, the alligator.

"I guess I'll see you tomorrow, friend. I should be heading back before this blizzard starts," Jeff said.

"See you tomorrow!" Todd replied.

As the two friends returned to their humble abodes, the first snowflake landed on the branch of an oak tree.

3.

"Coffee for Two"

By William R. Bartlett

Francis Albert MacPherson stepped into the restaurant and stopped at the greeter's station.

The young man behind the lectern lifted his head and beamed. "Welcome to Café 't'Amour. How many today?"

"Just the two of us."

The smile faltered as he looked over Mac's shoulder. "Um..."

"Rhys will be along in a minute."

The smile returned. "Of course. Would you like a booth or a table?"

"A booth, if you'd be so kind. With a view of the creek?"

"That shouldn't be a problem." The greeter glanced at the nearly empty dining room and pulled two laminated placards from the lectern. "This way, please." He led Mac to a nook near the window overlooking the steep, undeveloped gulley next to the parking lot and placed the menus on the table. "Enjoy your meal," he said and returned to the lectern.

Mac took off his coat and tossed it into the booth's corner.

A middle-aged woman stopped beside his table once he'd sat.

"Good afternoon, my name is Valerie, and I'm your server today. Can I get you anything to drink while you're deciding?"

"May we have a French vanilla latte with chicory for the lady and a cup of coffee for me, please? In fact, we won't be needing the menus. The drinks will be enough."

"Absolutely. I'll be right back." She took the placards from the table and glided away.

Mac sat on the padded bench and gazed at the empty space before him. *Anniversaries should be something special. A fancy dinner. Champagne. Flowers. They should be more than a cup of coffee.* He turned his head and glanced at the gully, teeming with unchecked plant life. Volunteer trees, weeds, wildflowers, and shrubs all competed for sunlight and soil. *Just not the same.*

"Here you go." Valerie took the latte off her tray and placed it opposite Mac, then set a coffee cup and an insulated pot before him. "Can I get you anything else?"

"No, thank you."

She glanced at the empty space. "If you'd like, I can bring a fresh latte in a few minutes. You know. In case she's… delayed."

"Thank you, that won't be necessary. I'm sure she'll be right here."

Valerie nodded. "Let me know if you need anything," she said before striding away.

Mac rubbed his eyes.

"Am I late?"

"Not terribly. Your absence was making the staff a little jumpy, though." He poured a cup of coffee. "I got your favorite."

"You goose." Rhys gave him a fond smile. "You know I can't drink that anymore."

"Old habits, I guess. Did you change your hair?"

"You're trying to suck up, aren't you?"

"No, seriously. Did you get it trimmed? Maybe add a little color?"

"Really, Mac? My hair hasn't changed in years. You should know that."

"I've always liked how you kept it short. Long enough to look feminine, but short enough to keep under control with little effort. I always thought it looked striking. Makes you easy to pick out in a crowd, too."

Rhys glanced at her coffee. "It's no good trying to butter me up. I'm not going home with you. Don't look at me like that, you know the reason."

"OK, I won't beg. But being the only person in the house just doesn't feel right." He took a sip of his coffee, glanced at the ravine, then back at Rhys. "I haven't stopped searching, you know."

"A fishing expedition isn't enough to get me home, I need answers. You're going to have to try harder. If you're lonely, find somebody else or get a dog."

"I *have* tried harder. Being with another woman would feel like cheating on you, and that's just not going to happen. I can't take care of a pooch, either, not with all my time spent on the inquiry in addition to work. It wouldn't be right."

"Have you tried asking around the neighborhood? Maybe somebody saw something."

"Twelve times. It's not a bad neighborhood, it's just that nobody was there when it happened. No matter what alley I take, every question I ask takes me to the same dead end."

She crossed her arms. "Science, then. You know, angles and velocities. That sort of thing."

"The authorities don't believe me. I've begged them to check, but, without anything conclusive from the coroner, I don't have a leg to stand on. They've written the whole thing off as a tragic accident and won't budge."

"Honestly, Mac, if you aren't going to try, there's no sense in pursuing this."

He slid his hands over the table toward her, but she kept her arms crossed. "I have an idea."

Rhys raised an eyebrow.

"I can get a metal detector and check out the ravine. The creek, too. If I can come up with some concrete evidence, maybe they'll listen."

"Why didn't you think of this years ago? Don't you want me home?"

His mouth tightened. "That's not fair, Rhys." He took his hands off the table and crossed his arms. "I stumbled onto a video about people using those tools to look for historical artifacts. We're looking for something small, so it's a long shot, but it may be the only hope we've got."

"Fine. Go get your gadgets and gizmos and do whatever you can."

"Come on, don't be like that. I know it's hard on you, but it's no picnic for me, either."

"You just don't understand."

"I know, and I won't be able to. Let's just make the best of it. Whaddaya say? Give me a smile, huh? Time was, you used to smile whenever I walked into the room."

Rhys gave him a steady look.

"OK, a horse walks into a bar and the bartender asks, 'Why the long face?"

She said nothing, but the corner of her mouth twitched.

"A man walked up to another man who was wearing a pendant that could have been a stylized anchor or a Norse hammer and asks, 'Is that an anchor or a hammer you have around your neck? The other guy says, 'It's a hammer.' 'Oh,' says the first guy, 'Does that mean you have a Thor throat?'"

Rhys chuckled, and the lines on her face eased. "Stop doing that. You're always making me laugh when I want to be mad at you."

"Just one small smile, then?"

Rhys grinned at him, just like their wedding photograph that still hung on his wall. "Happy?" Her face relaxed. "I have to go. Get your gear and do what you can. I'll see you later."

"No, don't leave. Not yet. Stay a bit longer."

"Sir?" Valerie's voice came from behind him. "Would you like me to warm up the latte?"

"No. No, thank you. If I could have the check, please?"

"You bet." Valerie scribbled on a piece of paper and laid it on the table. "It's a shame she couldn't make it. Most likely, something came up. Would you like me to get a to-go cup for you?"

"That won't be necessary but thank you for asking." He rose, pulled out his wallet and a few bills, well over double the check amount, and placed them on the table. "Thank you, Valerie, you've been very kind."

Mac pulled on his coat and strode out the door.

Valerie took the money and went to the cash register where she placed it in the till, stuffing the change into her pocket, then turned to Heather. "Did you see that? Poor schnook just got stood up. Got her a nice latte, too. Pity."

"That guy that just left? That's Mac. And he wasn't stood up." Heather took a deep breath. "His wife died several years ago when her car left the road and tumbled down that ravine."

"Oh, that's sad."

"Tell me about it. The police called it an accident, but Mac insists she was shot with a pellet gun while driving with her windows down."

"Are you saying one of those pea shooters could knock a car off the road? Really?"

"It's enough to distract her and make her lose control. The ravine and the creek did the rest."

"Did the police ever find any evidence she was shot?"

"Nope. An air rifle is quiet and doesn't have much range. It could even have been unintentional, like a kid shooting at tin cans across the creek, and she just happened to get in the way. I wish they'd reopen the case, maybe give him some closure. He's convinced me, but the investigators said that accidents happen and this was one. Mac comes in now and then and sits in that booth where he can look at the creek. That's where he was when it happened, waiting for her to show up for their anniversary lunch date. He saw the whole thing."

Valerie ran a damp cloth across the counter. "Does he always talk when he's alone in the booth?"

"I keep forgetting you're new here. Yeah, he talks. It was a little creepy at first, but he never raises a fuss, and he's always polite. Finally, I just stopped thinking about it. For all I know, he could be talking to his dead wife."

"Poor guy. You know, tragedies happen all the time, and you hear about 'em on the news, but when one up and hits you in the face... Maybe I should have been, well, a bit more friendly."

"You were fine. It's not like you knew and you were mocking him."

They stared toward the ravine.

Heather nudged Valerie and nodded toward a couple who'd just been seated. "You have another guest."

4.

"Tasteless"

By Kate Hampton

In bed, Claudia, a teenager, would slow down in the land of nod. Upon closing her eyes and activating her mind, she would see many different things- good or bad- in a massive window, into her subconscious mind.

Running around the meadows, Claudia felt the pearliness of the white petals peeping through the evergreen grass surrounding her. The sweet kisses of the daisies greeted her and made her lips split into a wide smile. She continued to walk through the center aisle. She embraced the sensational touches of the wind. That certain feel was just so dreamy—so perfect.

Whoa!

"I couldn't believe I'd see this for myself. This scene isn't a dream, right?" She asked herself with exhilarating joy. She was full of glee at that moment and did not want it to end.

Swish, swish, swish.

The golden rays of the sun gave dazzling hues to the sky. Claudia opened her eyes with a frowning face as the astonishing curtains caressed her skin. She wasted some seconds looking at the ceiling, trying to recall everything. She could still hear the beating of her heart. It looked like her dream was interrupted by the swishing sound she could hear from the outside. She decided to get up and check to see who was making this irritating sound that made her not enjoy her Saturday morning. As she expected, she saw her grandmother holding a broomstick, quiet and stern.

"Grandma, it's you again," she uttered and added, "How often did I tell you not to bother my sleep, especially during weekends?"

"I need to finish this; it's about to rain," her grandmother said, putting her full attention into finishing what she was doing.

Claudia rolled her eyes and turned away from her grandmother with unexplainable anger.

"I just want her to do it in the afternoon instead! Why does she always want to finish everything before I wake up? It's annoying!" Claudia kept mumbling as she found her way to the kitchen to prepare some hot drinks to appease her disappointment early in the morning.

When her grandmother appeared, she was about to pour hot water into her mug. Flabbergasted, she ended up hurting her fingers.

"Ouch!" she cried with pain and further said, "Your existence is suffocating. I can't stand this anymore."

"My dear Claudia, I already prepared your morning coffee. I'm sorry if I surprised you. I will be more careful from now on," Grandma Anne tried to assert herself in a loving tone.

"I always tell you I don't like you preparing my coffee every morning. Why do you keep on doing it? Is it that hard to comprehend?" she explained with glaring eyes toward her grandmother.

Her grandma looked sad and touched her heart.

"I don't like your coffee; it's tasteless!" Claudia emphasized.

Anne, her 80-year-old grandmother, just sat quietly, slumped on a couch, feeling deep dejection. She was old but still capable enough to do household chores. One of her routines was to keep their yard swept and neat. For some reason, busy or not, she was delighted to prepare her granddaughter's coffee every morning. She loved and cared for Claudia since birth, especially when her daughter died.

Living in the rural area had been easy for her, as she was used to a simple life. She would wake up at five o'clock. Then, she would get her antique copper kettle and put it on the wood-burning stove. Beside the stove, she would sit on her favourite bear-like wooden chair and wait until the water bubbled up ferociously. She was just so excited to prepare Claudia's morning brew. That was a simple thing she could do for her granddaughter to relieve her mind and heart. The time, care, comfort, and authenticity she invested could be seen in her simple effort. However, she would end up wasting it because Claudia wouldn't like to have a single sip of her coffee. Still, she remained persistent.

"I wish I could make her happy at the start of the day. I'm getting old, and I cannot tell what life will give me as the days pass by," Grandma Anne whispered.

Tick, tock, tick, tock...

As time ticked by, Claudia prepared and got dressed. She looked like a rose as she wore that red dress from her closet. She touched her lips with coral-red lipstick and brushed her hair. She had to leave before seven o'clock in the evening because she would attend her best friend's birthday party.

"Grandma, I'll be going to my best friend's house. I'll stay there for some time this evening. Please don't wait for me," Claudia shouted as she pulled the invitation card from her drawer and hurriedly put on her black shoes.

"Take care, dear Claudia!" Grandma Anne replied, noticing that her granddaughter didn't hear what she said.

Grandma Anne was left alone in their humble dwelling. She opted to enter Claudia's bedroom, and to her surprise, it was all a mess! Her clothes were everywhere. She didn't know where to start to clean up her granddaughter's room. That gave her a headache!

"I really hope she'll learn to take care of her things and keep them organized and tidy. What will she do if I'm already gone?" Grandma Anne remarked as what all grandmothers would naturally say to their granddaughters.

Grandma was cleaning Claudia's grubby things when she found a little pink box on her bed. She read the note written on a piece of paper.

"Happy Birthday, dearest Natalie! I hope you..."

Grandma rushed her way to the birthday party's venue. She couldn't even count her footsteps as she was in a hurry. She knew that it was something that Claudia would give her friend Natalie as a present.

Claudia was astonished by what she saw. She knew she would have a great time there with fancy decorations, glittering balls, and mouth-watering variety of dishes and desserts on the table.

"What's up, Claudia?" a girl from behind her uttered those words.

"Nats! This party looks so fun. Happy birthday, bestie! Here's my gi..."

Claudia searched for the gift inside her bag. She paused for a while, realizing she had gone to the party without the gift.

The silence broke when her grandmother came into her sight, weary and baggy.

"Did I just arrive at the right time? Dear, you left this gift at home," Grandma exclaimed while handing the pink box to Claudia.

"Oh, grandma, you're here!" Natalie hugged Grandma Anne and was very happy to see her at the party. Claudia, you didn't tell me your grandmother is coming, too!"

"Ah, I didn't expect her to be here as well," she replied.

"Oh, wait, grandma and bestie, just help yourselves out, and I hope you will both enjoy the party! I'll just go check on the other guests," Natalie remarked with a genuine smile.

"Grandma, do you really think I'm happy that you are here? Look at you and your worn-out clothes," Claudia cracked in anger.

"I found that pink box on your bed, and I thought heading here could at least help you. Aren't you grateful?" Grandma Anne asked and rubbed her head. Those exchanges of conversations triggered her headache once again.

"Do I look like I am?" Claudia murmured.

Grandma Anne couldn't take a single step from where she stood. She felt humiliated, thinking that Claudia did not acknowledge her effort. This incident aggravated her headache. She returned home with baffling emotions.

Moments passed, the party ended, and Claudia came home safely. She opened the door and saw her grandmother still wide awake, waiting for her to arrive. She didn't even take a glance at her and went straight to her bedroom, where she locked it. She grabbed her pillows, and with just five blinks of her eyes, she shut them and zoned out.

Another dawn had seeped. It was calm, and the place oozed with tranquility. Then, Claudia opened her eyes with perfect contentment. She did, indeed, sleep like a log last night.

She got up on her bed and moved the clean curtains on her windows. She saw no one outside. She was used to hearing some swishing sounds every day, but that particular morning was an exception.

"Maybe, she already realized how vexing it was to disturb someone's sleep in the morning," her thoughts came mumbling.

She went to the kitchen to prepare some hot drinks. No one else was there either. There was no hot drink from her grandmother this morning! She started to notice that she couldn't find her grandmother anywhere in the house. She thought that this day was special.

Claudia sat on a long bench outside their house and took a sip of her coffee. She consumed it and gleamed when she imagined the tasteless coffee of her grandmother.

"Where did grandma go?" she thought about this question for some time.

She was a bit worried about Anne. She decided to look for her, but she was nowhere to be found.

"Grandma! Grandma!" Claudia kept on shouting outside the house.

Her legs were shaking. She felt a sudden tightness in her chest. She couldn't see her. Oh no! Her grandma was missing!

Tears dripped from Claudia's eyes. She missed her grandmother so much. She kept on calling her grandma's name, but no one answered.

"Grandma, where are you? Please come home!"

The place remained silent. Claudia did not stop sobbing. She wanted to see her grandmother so badly.

All the things she did to her grandmother came flashing back. She was rude and disrespectful to her. She did not care for her. That's why she couldn't stop crying because she knew her grandmother loved her dearly. But she's gone now! Then, she realized how valuable Grandma Anne's existence was to her.

"I'm sorry, grandma! I'm sorry," she burst out with these words.

"Claudia, Claudia, wake up! You're dreaming!"

Claudia woke up from a nightmare when she heard Grandma Anne's soft voice.

She hugged her grandmother and cried out so loud. She continuously wept over her grandmothers' shoulders and apologized, "Grandma, you're here! I'm sorry!"

"Oh, dear Claudia, you were just having a nightmare. Shhhhh... You're fine now, stop crying," Grandma Anne said, stroking her hair to calm her.

It was all a dream- a good window in Claudia's mind was open. She understood and appreciated how important her grandmother had been to her all this time. She couldn't live without her. She was just so happy to see her grandma again.

"Get up; I already prepared your coffee," grandma uttered in a gentle tone.

Claudia rushed over to her grandmother. Together, they both went to the kitchen. The place's ambiance went back to what it used to be. The aroma of the coffee filled the air in their hot beverage station. She sat there and took a sip of the coffee that was poured and well-stirred on her favorite mug.

"Grandma, why is this still tasteless?" she added jokingly. At the back of her mind, nothing was as tasteless as she could ever feel if she couldn't see her grandmother again.

Grandma Anne just smiled and replied, "I know you like it now."

They both just laughed, and they continued catching up. Claudia repeated her nightmare to her grandmother. Grandma Anne just listened to her granddaughter's story and felt perfect happiness inside.

Grandma said, "People say that sometimes when you're in a land of nod or simply in the state of sleep, your window of dreams becomes a reality."

"But I don't want to happen such kind of land of nod; that's too profound for me," Claudia remarked and sipped her coffee.

"Still tasteless?" Grandma asked.

"'Tis the best coffee!" Claudia said and kissed her beloved grandma.

5.

"Celestine's Perfect Coffee Mate"

By Josephine Go

"Good morning, Arizona!"

Celestine felt so blessed, waking up this morning, looking at the glorious sun, rising and basking in the splendor of the Divine's beautiful creations. She was so thankful that she woke up again for another day and survived the work as a caregiver at the assisted living home that has become her residence since she arrived from the Philippines.

"Ouch, my back hurts a bit from yesterday's work," she whispered to herself.

She did a mental review of what was in store for the day: Four ambulants and one dead-weight elderly. She had to be on her toes all the time, ensuring that the elderlies were all well-taken care of and provided with their needs.

She opened her schedule notebook. She looked at the many previous entries. A seminar in a caregiving course, as required by the Arizona State Law, was set on a particular Wednesday. Still vivid in her mind, she remembered scribbling those words.

"How did I juggle this insane schedule?" Celestine shook her head but gently smiled.

It was all a far cry from what she used to do in the Philippines. She had a hard time adjusting at first, being far from her family and suffering homesickness every day.

She agonized over her husband's absence. He has been her constant partner. She called him her break time buddy.

"Coffee breaks without my sweetheart are so different," at home, she said and turned to touch the picture frame, standing on a beside table. She gingerly caressed the photo of her husband. She could almost hear their conversations about the family's move to Arizona.

"I'm not sure if this job is for me without you."

Her husband was reluctant to leave his job and change his career. He is the type of person who does not want to take risks. He loved his job as a building administrator, which he held for fifteen years.

"The kids are in their teens. They have their roots here. They are happy with the school and their friends," her sweetheart explained.

Celestine understood him. They have all worked hard and built a beautiful life together. She knew it was tough for him to let go of what they had already achieved.

In retrospect, his kiss still lingered on her cheek. She called to mind that he did not say goodbye. Instead, he clearly said, "I will see you soon." She could see his hesitance and worried look when he told her to call him upon her arrival in Arizona. Celestine had mixed feelings then. She was concerned and a bit anxious but very excited at the same time.

Celestine walked to the kitchen and poured herself a cup of coffee. She fondly recalled how she slowly became comfortable in her new surroundings.

First, she met James, who was a very fun-loving driver who would drive her to different facilities. James is the son of Celestine's employer. The kind lady and her family own seven facilities. It was she who knew the ropes of the business. James also said that his mother would be the one to brief her on everything she needed to know about the job.

She felt a bit amused, reminiscing about her first assignment in Scottsdale. She recalled feeling a bit jittery, but full of excitement.

Liza was the second person she met at work. She was the first resource person and obviously helped her go through her newfound job. "Sweet Liza," she uttered.

During these times, Celestine did not have moments to feel homesick and sad. She was so tired that she fell fast asleep as soon as her head touched the pillow. Her duties and chores were exhausting, and the elderlies were all the dead weight that required body lifting. Still, she found her new job challenging and a new adventure to experience.

Adapting to her new job became easier because her co-workers were all Filipinos. They welcomed her and introduced her to their circles of friends in the Filipino Community.

But not long after, Celestine began to feel the not-so-friendly atmosphere with some of her co-workers. Sadly, she accepted the fact that not everyone could be her friend. Even though she tried to be as accommodating as she could, there was still something lacking to get their friendship. At that time, she had no right to judge and discriminate against them, so she just kept her distance and treated them as civilly as she could. She tried not to have enemies among her co-workers and decided that she would not stay at the facility longer than she should.

Celestine browsed through another page of her daily schedule. The words "Congrats, Manager!" were scribbled. This happened three weeks after she earned her Certificate in Caregiving and Certificate in Managing Care Home. She was assigned as Manager of one of the Facilities in Scottsdale. She thanked her employer for trusting her with such a position and promised to do her best as the new Manager of the Facility. She realized then why she earned the ire of some co-workers.

"Be careful, you got the position you wanted so much, but this can cause you more enemies," her husband told her.

Once again, even though her husband is far away, he remains her best buddy and her dearest coffee mate.

Then, one day, Celestine's husband suddenly called her and told her that he was having problems with his job. He wanted to resign and was thinking about her proposal. This issue gave her hope, and she waited for him to finalize his decision.

Again, she knew how hard it was for him to let go of some of their properties. He seemed attached to their van and car, which they bought with hard-earned money. But when she told him that they could acquire more cars in Arizona and even buy a house eventually, he seemed more encouraged to pursue their plans.

Celestine and her children were so happy and excited. She was dazed at first because everything happened so fast and so soon.

For more than three weeks, she was alone. Then suddenly, her whole family will be joining her in the near future.

"Hubby starts with his job" was another entry she read. She lovingly touched the words that she had scribbled. She felt so grateful that her own employer offered her coffee mate a job at the facility as well.

Things would be easier for her then because she could easily train her husband on what to do, and they would be partners in everything. She felt so happy and grateful because in time she and her husband would be coffee mates again in doing everything.

After hearing the job offer from Celestine's employer, her husband said yes and told her that he was actually thinking of applying as a caregiver. This made

Celestine very happy upon learning that her husband was prepared to work with her.

Later, Celestine looked at the table across the room and saw more photo frames. Then, she imagined the whole family standing in front of a beautiful house. She felt quite emotional.

With her employer vouching for her, she was able to rent a house with a pool very near the facility where they would be assigned.

She looked at that picture closely. She thought of the van that would be parked at the corner of the photo. She giggled, knowing the van could make her husband happy.

In their last conversation on the phone, before the family flew to Arizona, the children asked their mom what they wanted them to bring her.

"All of you and your dad to be here in Arizona. That is all I need." Celestine almost choked, trying to control her tears.

Ere long, all of them arrived. Days passed and in a short time, the family had lots of time to catch up and adjust to the new environment.

Without delay for the children's schooling, the school bus came to fetch them. Celestine's children rushed to kiss her goodbye and headed off to school.

"Care for another cup? But wait, do you want it from the one you brewed, or from one of these instant coffee packs that your children brought you back from home?" her husband asked as he reached for his own mug.

Celestine's eyes widened with glee. She did not know that when the children asked what she wanted, they really meant to bring her something. She said all she needed was for them to come, yet they brought some of her favorite coffee.

"The one from home, of course! I was just waiting to drink my second cup with you, coffee mate!" She nudged him a bit, then lovingly leaned her head on his shoulder.

6.

"No Sugar, Please!"

By Lucy Lombos

Bzzzt, bzzzt, bzzzt! The table clock rang, alarming at six o'clock in the morning inside a dim bedroom. A hand groped to touch and grabbed it to stop its apparently screaming sound, as anybody would imagine and feel annoyed. Although still sleepy, it was time to get up on that particular weekday, Friday the thirteenth.

The sun came out as if the galaxy king would like to greet this cheerful woman ahead of other well-wishers. She would turn 60 soon, so reaching this diamond celebration is quite a milestone.

"Family members and close friends are coming on Sunday. There are some things I need to get from the attic. But what better way to drink coffee first and reminisce about the past," Liz, the soon-to-be celebrant and the well-accomplished senior citizen, thought with a bright smile. It showed her two dimples.

One of her fondest memories came back to her and she almost saw it in front of her. Cenen, her childhood bosom buddy, was a sweet young girl she met in a rural village named Lazareto.

The village community looked small yet populous of both the rich and the marginalized families. However, everyone displayed the spirit of warmth, friendliness, and hospitality. Days of yore, most people had to familiarize themselves with each other for health and well-being support, and livelihood assistance.

Since childhood, Liz and Cenen immediately clicked. The twain loved to laugh at jokes, walk to school together, and help each other with schoolwork and household chores. They knew they were both gifted with good singing voices, so they sang with the church choir. Known in the community because of their looks and pleasing personalities, people invited them to "flower pinning" dances, attend parties and religious events.

Volunteering was their other activity. They would clean the Black Nazarene Chapel every Saturday afternoon before the Sunday early mass would be officiated by the parish priest. That duty became their weekend routine that turned into fun, like they were only playing at the chapel.

All year round, rain or shine, one of the cultural practices in that neighborhood was paying the last respect for and viewing the dead. When someone died, everyone would try to attend the wake and participate in the funeral schedule of activities and services. Often, the viewing is set at the house to avoid the hefty amount the funeral chapels or parlors charge. The wake usually lasts a number of days, and the burial is also costly. Hence, expenses increase.

In Lazareto, the wake would eventually incline into a social gathering for family and close friends—whatever social status people might have. Sometimes, those nights would also be opportunities to pay court to and woo lovely ladies in the village.

Men would spot the fairest women.

"Hi, Liz! How are you? May I visit you tomorrow evening at six o'clock?" Leo greeted and advanced into some romantic introduction.

"Hi! Sorry, I am busy at school. It's our periodic exam. I have no time for such a thing," Liz turned down Leo's initial move to court her.

Quite embarrassed, that guy who had not finished a college degree, yet owned a farm, would only strum his guitar and sing *"Minsan Lang."* It was his composition, translated into English as something like "Just Once in this Life." It was incredibly dedicated to Liz.

Cenen, always in a sunny disposition, would only giggle whenever Liz said no. She knew Liz's dream man-tall, handsome, professional and from a foreign country. The two women would talk about their castles in the air and share their interests and secrets even at funeral wakes.

One of the things that people look forward to at funerals in this community is the food that would be served. Usually, biscuits, bread or sandwiches, candies, sodas and cups of coffee would overflow.

*** *** ***

Liz roused from her daydreaming as soon as she thought of coffee. She stood up to fetch a freshly brewed cup.

Without a doubt, Liz was a coffee lover. It was coffee that would kickstart her day. Funny, but it was the very first thing in the morning that she would do, aside from washing her face, combing her hair and brushing her teeth.

Coffee, an everyday tonic lifeline, would pop into her mind and rhythmically throb in her heart! Young in mind and spirit, she loved to stir her coffee playfully, creating the beautiful clinking sound of the teaspoon against the breakable cup. The sound usually generated a piece of enlivening music for her. To wake her up, in addition, she would enjoy slurping her brewed drink. After drinking the first round of the morning beverages, she would wash the cup and prepare for her noble teaching job.

Liz evolved as an author of children's books after teaching elementary students for years. As a writer, she always craved coffee. For her, it was best for a cup to be positioned in front of her right hand for an easy grab. Her bright early day and snack time in the afternoon would only be completed by drinking a brewed one, whatsoever the season would be.

For Liz, her roasted bean juice did not only represent a cup of hot stuff that stimulated her brain in an instant. She remarked, "It's also a status symbol but with worthwhile sense and engagement. It relates to alertness concerning my job."

Her work made her think of realities, truths, practical observances, and sometimes abstract and ingenious notions. For that reason, coffee became her work's uncomplaining pal as if she could interact with it. Often, she called it her brain juice to do excellent thinking for her writing projects.

Without fail, Liz preferred not only steaming as though still in flames, but black coffee! She hated milk. Well, making it black only meant the intended purpose of having a strong and sharp taste. Its aroma awakened her more when she sipped it right away. As her first-rate love, a cuppa of black coffee activated her mental cognition creativities. Beyond that, it added up to something that matched her hardship or struggle in writing. Slim and feebly looking as she was, writing was her therapy, an expression of herself. Moreover, she thought its bitterness would make her robust and could fight her daily battle.

Indeed, for Liz, black coffee also represented her simplicity because it only comprised two ingredients available in the neighborhood- ground coffee and clean water from the backyard's well- as simple as that!... And presto! She had a breakfast energy drink with a short time of preparation. In other words, as a phenom, she would drink lots of this fluid intelligence in a row with no sweetener because it was easy and quick to make.

Furthermore, she started the practice of drinking what she fondly called the "Lizzy kind of coffee" when she was young, at around five years old. So, it could already be considered something like a stimulant-addiction. She was clearly influenced by her family. They all loved black coffee in the morning and throughout the day. Coming from a low-income family, twinning black coffee with bread became a happy treat and an afternoon delight for all.

The top influencer on drinking Asian coffee was her grandmother, whom she called with love and respect as Lola Inna.

Lola Inna would tag Liz along on her trips to the grocery shops. A special one was owned by Liz's great-grandmother, from where they would buy ground coffee for only five cents. The ground beans and fantastic smell amazed the young girl in Liz. Her great-grandmother would place the ground coffee in "balisusong papel," a coned paper in English. There was no abundant and fancy coffee bean container then in the 60s but paper, commonly recycled newspaper or brown paper. Yeah, life was a lot simpler in those years than nowadays!

Lovingly, Lola Inna would always continue brewing coffee and offer one to her granddaughter. Years went on with that drinking mode, already a second nature to mark. Even when Liz felt feverish, she would drink piquant coffee which gave her an appetizing taste to eat food, renewed strength, and, eventually, healing. But there was one thing she would simply request and wished to be always remembered and held dear.

"No sugar, please!" Liz said when asked how she wanted her coffee. She favored it that way. Remember,

Liz and coffee with no sugar would ring a bell like mighty combined life partners.

How did it all start that Liz's coffee should be plain and not sweet? Because Liz got sick. It was a lifetime illness. She has had diabetes since she was still like a fledging bird.

However industrious Liz was, and sometimes not feeling well, occasionally, when there was a wake in the community, she would attend the viewing and see who breathed their last. Together with her Lola Inna, she also uttered prayers for the dead. She learned that all souls and departed loved ones should be offered prayers and holy masses for the souls' eternal peace.

Many times, Liz would bring Cenen along with her to attend the wake of those who passed away. Attending funeral vigils at night would say a lot about Filipino culture. Significantly, it manifested paying their final respect to the family member or anyone who had been known, and the same with an ordinary member of the community.

After praying, reading the biblical passage and paying attention to the bereaved family members' and the renowned people's eulogies, Liz and Cenen could chat with other funeral attendees, hearing the latest gossips. They would be enjoying their company and laughing out loud because of the jokes shared by all. They also joined in karaoke singing, playing cards, local table card games, and many more.

Traditionally important in the vigil was serving hot cups of coffee; purposely because people should be awake till midnight to watch over the dead and observe the surrounding. Moreover, coffee was also regarded as the cheapest beverage to serve the people. And so, Liz and Cenen would have rounds of free hot stuff.

"Ahh, so aromatic!" Liz smelled her favorite thing in the world.

But for Cenen, she preferred latte coffee and would sip it under her breath. Precisely the opposite of Liz!

"This is my kind of coffee. With milk!" Cenen said.

Every now and then, she would tease Liz by adding a teaspoon of sugar in her best friend's coffee cup.

"Oh, you're naughty!" Liz retorted while Cenen would only giggle.

While drinking coffee, these two women would consider funeral wakes as carefree times to bond with each other and relax. They wouldn't know the time when they were together. Aside from that, they would admire the decorated coffin with the flowers and lights adorned in the funeral home. Names of the mourning family were attached to the coffin's top and open cover. With eschatological acceptance in their beliefs, this wake was the last of the demised person's milestones and described as the celebration of life.

*** *** ***

As Liz took the last sip from her cup, she realized that time had flown by. Lots of things should be done before her birthday. Off to the attic, she went to grab the things she had earlier told herself that she needed. She knew she would have to use a ladder, so she went to Cenen to borrow one.

When she was about to start, the power suddenly shut off. While waiting, a fellow author-friend whom she met from a writing convention called. They had a long chat, and she greeted Liz for her coming birthday.

"It seemed something was hindering me from going to the attic," Liz expressed.

Shortly after, she was able to go up to the attic. After her last step from the ladder, she took a whiff of the musty odor. She went all the way up and hit the light switch. Oh, it all looked dusty! The moths sheltered themselves in the powdery dirt particles. Thick cobwebs were hanging. Standing against the wall was a reliable broom. She tried to remove the cobwebs when she caught sight of a huge spider.

She swung the broom to hit the giant arachnid. This extraordinary, eight-legged insect saw her and quickly moved. It tried to save its own life but probably on second thought, it approached her, ready with its venomous fangs. It crawled and jumped onto her neck!

The spider was able to escape. Feeling frightened and exhausted, Liz decided to get down from the ladder. In a few minutes, she suddenly felt dizzy while the insect became invisible at that moment. It ensconced itself in a staunch structure. Away from Liz's view, it nestled in a hidden strategy at its newly created web made of silk threads, with remaining high energy around its new victim.

With queasy feeling, Liz lay down on the floor. "What a horrible nightmare!" she mumbled as she tried to pull herself together. Somehow, she felt unable to move and had a hard time breathing. She felt so tired and decided to stay there and take a nap.

The following day, Liz heard that someone had died. The wake was located at the hilly part of the village. Everyone went up the hill where the dead was temporarily laid.

Liz felt that she wasn't herself and wished Cenen could go on her behalf.

Every time Liz moved, she felt exhausted. "Was it because of a high sugar level again?" she surmised.

She started to miss her best friend, whom she sensed might be already looking for her. She looked down at her arms. Her skin was strangely pale.

"What happened to Cenen? She didn't bother to tell me if she was going there or not?" Liz wondered.

By all means, on the day of rest, she brushed her hair, twisted it and wrapped into a low bun. Then, she put on her simple make-up, wore a long, white dress, and covered herself with an ashen-white shawl. She tried to smile; her dimples didn't appear. Alone, somewhat sick and sallow, she went to the funeral locale.

Family and friends, lots of people from far and wide, including her co-teachers and students, and her fellow authors, attended the wake. Leo, who did not get married, played the guitar and sang *"Minsan Lang"*. Her other former male suitors showed up, too in mourning mood.

Yet, no one was leading the prayer. In an instant, Liz missed her Lola Inna.

Then, she saw someone holding coffee beans in a coned paper- the "balisusong papel." Of course, someone was in charge of brewing coffee. She smelled its aroma once again.

"Ahh, superb!" Liz commented like an addict who was dependent on a particular substance.

Servers began distributing and offering cups of black coffee.

"No sugar, please!" she requested.

But the server did not notice her. She began to feel ignored.

Brushing off this gloominess in her heart, she looked for her best friend. At last, she found her sitting on one of the white chairs. But Cenen was crying.

"Why?" she started to get puzzled.

Another server came around, offering cups of black coffee.

After that, she heard Cenen saying with tears to the server, "No sugar, please!"

"Oh my, Cenen has learned to love the unsweetened coffee!" Liz remarked and smiled, showing her dimples, yet they looked deepened with loosened muscles.

Her buddy stirred the hot coffee, producing a playful sound, and slurped it as she would.

"Hey, that's me!"

Liz, too, would like to get one cup and indulge. But no one seemed to hear her requests.

"Hello, Cenen! Why are you crying? Are you alright?" she tried to converse with her best friend. She did not hear a single reply. So, she just sat beside her, mouth shut, waiting to get her attention.

Some funeral attendees began to slice and taste the lovely cake on the back table. Weird! A few also sang the birthday song.

"Whose birthday is it?" in silence, Liz questioned.

On the contrary, Cenen kept sobbing and Liz wondered why.

After several minutes, already bored and out of curiosity, Liz approached the silvery white coffin. It was well-polished and had diamond-glimmering lines around it. Scented candles around the place were all in glittering diamond shades. Flowers looked gorgeous. She read the names of the family members, written in blue strips of ribbons and attached to the coffin's well-adorned top cover. Then, she discovered that the names all belonged to her dearly beloved family. And her name wasn't there!

"Oh no!" she finally understood. She touched her neck and remembered the giant spider. Scary!... She looked at the person in the coffin. "I am now peacefully asleep. And yes, they are celebrating my birthday, too!" Even if she felt she uttered these sentences aloud, no one had heard her. She felt somehow empty. She was sorrowful. Her tears began to fall, albeit she accepted her fate.

The time had come, just like the alarm clock buzzing to wake her. Bzzzt! Bzzzt! Bzzzt! Time to go... life was over. She already passed on! She recalled her phobia of the killer spider and how it bit her. She lost consciousness right after that fatal incident. Yet, this time without fear of anything, she said, "I must go to my Creator!"

Forever after, she would cross over to a better place. Well, no choice! But before that, she glimpsed for the last time at her birthplace, Cenen, and her coffee with no sugar. She gently kissed and thanked her childhood buddy. She also whispered something.

"Cenen, you sweetened my life and, yes, my coffee."

The Author

Hi! **Lucy E. Lombos** is the primary author of this book- a collection of short stories.

Each letter of her first name has meaning.

L- Light. Yes, that's right, the bubbly light of the family! She is a loving daughter and sister, a wife, a mom of three sweethopes, a grandma of her first sweetjoy, a jolly friend and a dedicated teacher. She always asks the Holy Spirit to enlighten her mind, to inspire her and guide her all the time. Praise God! Modesty aside, she graduated with Honors- Valedictorian in Elementary, Silver Medalist with General Excellence Award in High School and Cum Laude in College. She had a religious education and formation at Don Bosco Seminary College, and graduated at the Divine Word College of Calapan, SVD. In De La Salle University, Taft, Manila, she pursued her graduate studies; and completed the academic units at the University of the Philippines where she specialized in Language and Literacy. She further enhanced her English proficiency skills by enrolling in TESOL (Teaching English to Speakers of Other Languages) with Practicum Course in British Columbia, Canada where she obtained a very high grade.

U- Understanding. She has a substantial and deep understanding of her profession. She undertakes teaching the English fundamental skills, and these are – Speaking, Reading, Writing and Listening. In 2000, she founded Lombosco

Academy in the Philippines and she remains the Academy Directress, and the Editor-In-Chief of its Newsletter.

C- Children. They are the subject of her craft. She studied courses about Writing for Children and Writing a Life Story in Canada. She also earned a Diploma in Child Psychology in USA. Her love for children doesn't stop, and so she studied Child Protection: Children's Rights in Theory and Practice, an online course in Harvard University during the peak of the Covid-19 pandemic.

Y- Young. She is always young at heart. She would like to learn more, that's why she never stops resting on her laurels. Further, she is a member of SCBWI- Society of Children's Book Writers and Illustrators, ILA- International Literacy Association and CCCF- Canadian Child Care Federation. She also enjoys blogging, contributing articles for different media and doing educational vlogs.

*N.B. *Lucy taught at Puerto Galera Academy after her College Graduation; and became the Principal at Prince of Peace Montessori, Puerto Galera.* *She received two, official recognitions for promoting the Tourism in Puerto Galera, Or. Mindoro, Philippines to the International Level through her authored books in March 2018, and in the following year. **On February 26, 2023, she became a Finalist in the 2023 Woman of Worth Worldwide, held in Marriott Hotel, Burnaby, BC, Canada. Exactly after one month, she was featured in the Gallery Walk for the 77th SVD's Founding Anniversary.*

Bibliography

Lucy Lombos' Published Books on Amazon

1. *Ang Tinago Kong Piso/The Peso-Coin I Kept (Bilingual)*
2. *The Class Lady Bug*
3. *The Star of the Sea: A Boat Ride*
4. *Happiness 365 and ¼ Days (a biography)*
5. *'Ter and Ter', the Turtle and the Eagle*
6. *The Joys of Junior*
7. *Swanie's Bag*
8. *Rose of Calapan (a novel)*
9. *Bono (an early chapter book)*
10. *Three Fables, Part 1: Keys to Change the Heart*
11. *Three Fables, Part 2: Sparks to Brighten One's Purpose in Life*
12. *Pinky Oinky*
13. *Gracie and Dots*
14. *Noshi*
15. *After Six o' Clock Nightfall (short stories quadrilogy)*
16. *One Drop, Two Drops and Much More*
17. *Ellie-Phant and Mon-Keysha*
18. *Monsters in Lazareto (folktales)*
19. *Ely's Gift (an early chapter book)*
20. *Cotton and Nibbles*
21. *Beary G*
22. *Love, Fishbeak*
23. *Like the Sand and Like the Living Rock (a coloring book for kids)*
24. *Wednesday*

25. *Solana*
26. *The String of Saga Seeds (a novel)*
27. *Wiz Jordy's Magic Words*
28. *Rock Bottom Stories and Prayers (religious and inspirational)*
29. *Caffeinated Short Stories – the book you are reading.*
30. *Contributor to Theresa Jacobs' Self-Help Book: Writing 101, How to Write for Yourself & Share with the World.*

***** Her upcoming books- *****

31. *Peachy and Pinky ~Purring Together~*
32. *Echo and Light Poetry Anthology*

Theresa Jacob's Published Books on Amazon

Novels

Cataclysm
Kept
The Used
Handsome (Detective Gagon Book 1)
The Cleaner (Detective Gagon Book 2)

Novellas

Sudden Death
The Cimmerians
Wife N' Death
The Zombie Effect
The Guardian
Unfamiliar Territory
Into The Salton Sea
The Ghost in Me (Spring 2023)

Anthologies

Shrouded Voices
Things only the Darkness Knows
My Other Friends & More Stories
100-Word Horrors Books 1, 2, 3, 4.
A World Unimagined
Indie Writers Review Issue 13
Elements of Horror: Vol.1 Air, Vol.2 Earth, Vol.3 Water.
The Weird and What Not
A Discovery of Writers
Depth of Darkness
A is for Aliens
The Horror Zine's Book of Ghost Stories
Flashbulb Moment
Glimmer
It Came from Darkness
Time After Time
The Horror Zine Spring Edition
After Six O'clock Nightfall
The Horror Zines Book of Werewolf Stories
Fear the Forge

Kids' Books

The Lonely Leaf
Puddle Jumping

Poetry

Spewed Thoughts

Self-Help

Writing 101, How to Write for Yourself & Share with the World.
Yours to Write, Story Prompt Notebook.

William R. Bartlett's Published Books on Amazon

I. Nude, Light Housekeeping (a novel)
II. Tales from the Frozen North (an anthology): His contributions are-
1) The Island
2) A Paragon of Virtue
III. Welcome to Effham Falls (an anthology): His contribution is-
1) Two Arrowheads

Max H.'s Published Book on Amazon

I. Rock Bottom Stories and Prayers (religious and inspirational)- Her contribution's title is-
1) The Pit

Josephine Go's Published Book on Amazon

I. Rock Bottom Stories and Prayers (religious and inspirational)- Her contribution's title is-
1) Saved!

The Major Sponsors

LOMBOSCO ACADEMY FOUNDATION, INC.

Since 2000

Telephone numbers: 8842-7992; 8842-6519

Address:
11 C. Arellano St/, Phase 1, Katarungan Village,
Poblacion, Muntinlupa City, Metro Manila.

MAGNIFICAN IMMIGRATION AGENCY

Website: https://magnificanimmigration.com/
Email: info@magnificanimmigration.com

Acknowledgment

I would like to express my deep gratitude to the following people for giving me the big support which I humbly needed in writing this book –

Umberto Lombos, Jr. for publishing this book;

Annie Datu-Enriquez for copyediting the stories;

Ely, my mom and the entire family for giving me the moral support in my writing ministry;

To the following writer-contributors in this book,

their surnames were written based on the dates of their submission-

Theresa Jacobs, Maxine Hernandez, William R. Bartlett,

Kate Hampton and Josephine Go;

To the blurb writers,

Alexander Martin Pozon,

Maria Nancy A. Cayanan,

and

Daniel D. Enriquez...

I am truly amazed and grateful to you all.

***

The proceeds of the book sales are intended for a private school foundation and other public charities in the Philippines.

www.ingramcontent.com/pod-product-compliance
Lightning Source LLC
LaVergne TN
LVHW010940110826
845149LV00013B/2693

* 9 7 8 1 9 9 0 2 9 6 1 2 3 *